CARTOONING TRICKS

Ajit Narayan

SCHOLASTIC
New York Toronto London Auckland
Sydney New Delhi Hong Kong

Published by Scholastic India Pvt. Ltd.
A subsidiary of Scholastic Inc., New York, 10012 (USA).
Publishers since 1920, with international operations in Canada, Australia, New Zealand, the United Kingdom, India, and Hong Kong.

For information regarding permission, write to:
Scholastic India Pvt. Ltd.
A-27, Ground Floor, Bharti Sigma Centre,
Infocity-I, Sector-34, Gurgaon 122001 (India).

First edition: August 2014
Reprinted: September ; October ; December 2014; January; March:
sJune 2015 ; March; May 2016; January 2017 ; December 2018 ; 2022

ISBN-13: 978-893-5103-319-6

Printed by Shivam Offset Press, New Delhi

ABOUT THE AUTHOR

AJIT NARAYAN IS A WELL-KNOWN CARTOONIST AND HAS BEEN A WORKSHOP CONSULTANT FOR OVER 20 YEARS. HE IS ALSO THE AUTHOR OF SEVERAL INSTRUCTIONAL BOOKS ON CARTOONING.

CONTENTS

CARTOON FIGURES	2
BALANCE	3
POSES	6
MOVEMENTS	12
DIRECTIONAL MOVEMENTS	17
MOVEMENTS WITH REASONS	22
ACTION POSES	30
DISTORTIONS	36
ANIMALS IN MOTION	46
INANIMATE OBJECTS	51
SPEECH BALLOONS	54
SPECIAL EFFECTS	57

INTRODUCTION

ONCE YOU HAVE LEARNT TO DRAW BASIC CARTOON FIGURES, THE NEXT STEP IS TO BRING YOUR FIGURES TO LIFE THROUGH SPECIAL TECHNIQUES THAT COMMUNICATE SOUND AND MOVEMENT.

IN THIS BOOK, YOU WILL LEARN TO APPLY THESE TECHNIQUES TO YOUR OWN CARTOONS.

CARTOON FIGURES

THE CORE ESSENTIAL IN ALMOST ANY CARTOON IDEA IS A CHARACTER OR A FIGURE.

THE KEY TO UNDERSTANDING HOW THE HUMAN BODY MOVES IS THROUGH OBSERVATION.

START BY DRAWING A MATCHSTICK FIGURE. IF DRAWN CORRECTLY, IT WILL ALWAYS CREATE THE STANDARD BODY PROPORTIONS.

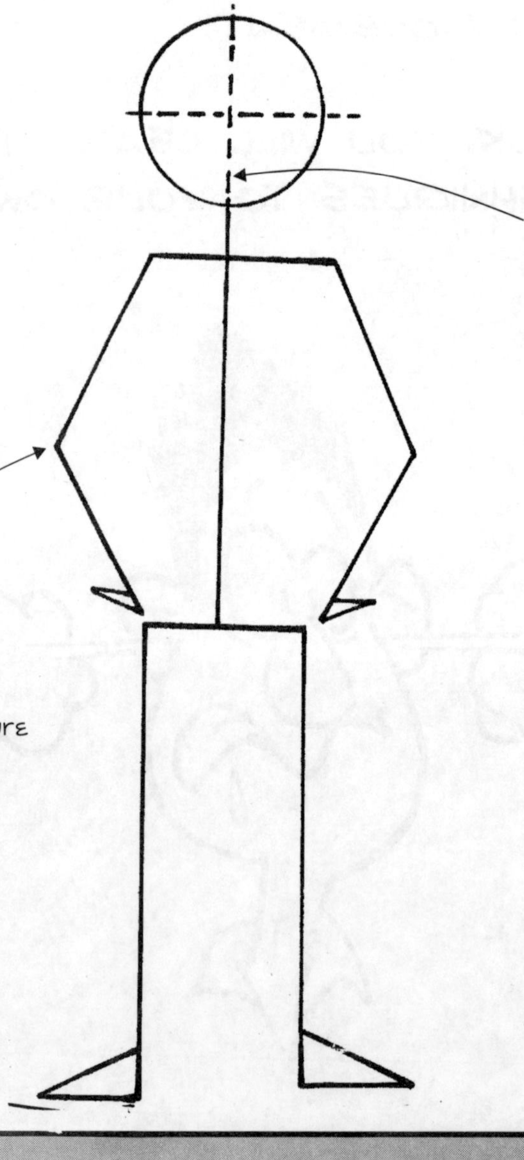

Draw a vertical line through the centre of the body so that there are two equal parts. This will help create the right tilt.

Think about the joints in the body, such as the elbows, the knees and the heels, and picture how they move.

BALANCE

ESTABLISH YOUR POINT OF SUPPORT—DRAW A VERTICAL LINE FROM THE BASE OF THE CHARACTER'S NECK TO THE HEEL OF THE LEG THAT IS FIRMLY PLACED ON THE GROUND OR SOMEWHERE BETWEEN THE FEET.

Make sure that half of the character's body weight is on one side of the line and half on the other.

If the figure is carrying an object like a cricket bat, then make sure the reader feels the strain or the weight of the bat.

POSES

THE POSES OF CARTOON CHARACTERS GIVE YOU A CLUE ABOUT WHO THEY ARE AND WHAT THEY ARE DOING.

TO BRING YOUR CHARACTER TO LIFE, YOU NEED TO CREATE A MOVABLE FRAME BY DRAWING STICK FIGURES. THIS STICK FIGURE FRAME WILL FORM THE BASE ON WHICH YOU WILL BUILD UP YOUR CARTOON CHARACTER.

MAKE SURE YOU SKETCH CHARACTERS IN ACTIVE POSITIONS OR POSTURES. IF YOU WISH TO BREATHE LIFE INTO YOUR CHARACTERS, ARRANGE THEIR LEGS, ARMS AND BODY ANGLES IN THE RIGHT POSITIONS.

ONCE YOU ARE SATISFIED WITH THE WAY YOUR FINAL DRAWING HAS TURNED OUT, YOU CAN ERASE THE STICK FIGURE.

THE FOLLOWING ARE A VARIETY OF POSES TO GET YOU STARTED.

LEAPING

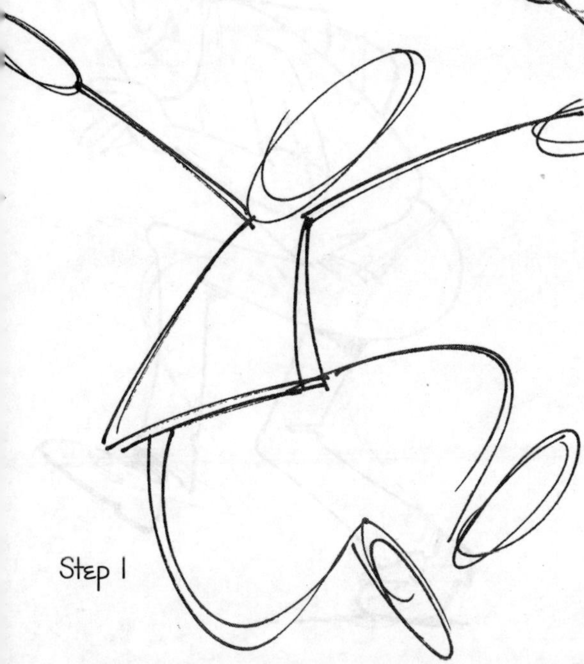

Step 1

Step 2

Step 3

Body stretched out, arms raised and an upward sweep of legs will bring about the right leaping effect.

SNEAKING

The weight of the entire body shifts to the left foot, showing eagerness and stealth.

FALLING

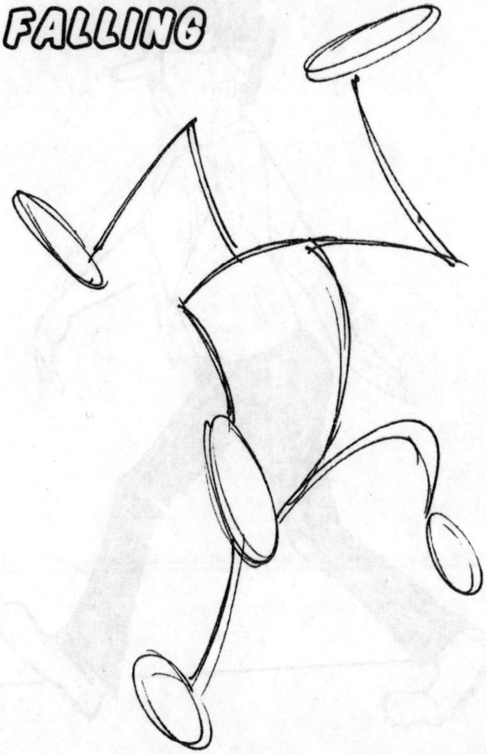

This figure is depicting an expression of shock, with flailing arms and legs. The body appears to be in a state of free fall.

WALKING

The hands and feet are placed in a symmetrical manner, the body weight equally balanced on both sides.

SITTING

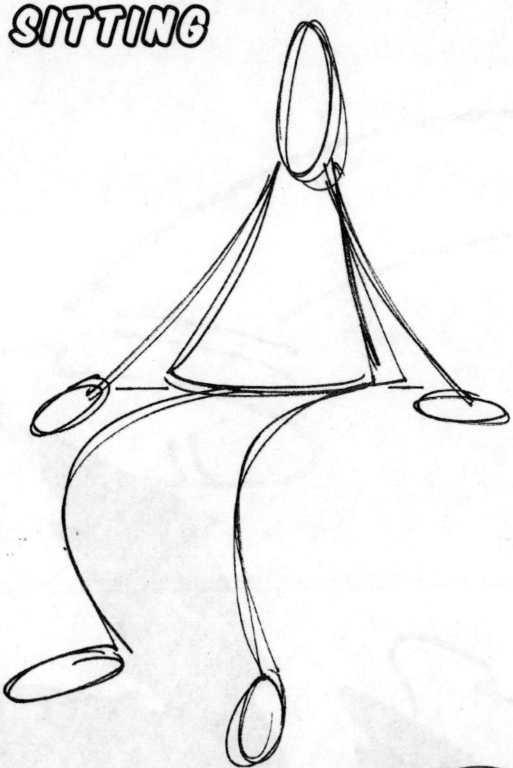

The legs are drawn at an angle to the body with the arms on the sides, showing a relaxed seated posture.

MOVEMENTS

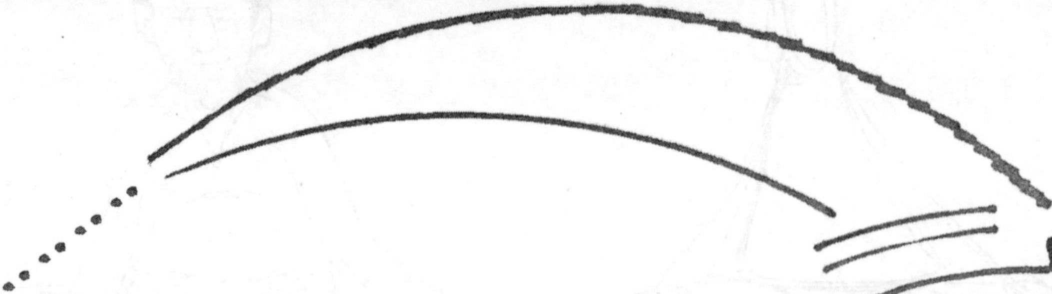

A CARTOONIST'S REAL TALENT LIES IN MAKING THE READER SEE AND FEEL A MOVEMENT THAT IS TAKING PLACE. THE 'MOTION LINE' IS A POPULAR TOOL THAT HELPS ACHIEVE THIS OBJECTIVE. IT COMPRISES LINES DRAWN AROUND THE OBJECTS IN MOTION. MOTION LINES SHOULD BE USED CAREFULLY AND ONLY WHERE ABSOLUTELY RELEVANT. IF YOU USE THEM APPROPRIATELY, YOUR FIGURES WILL COME TO LIFE.

REMEMBER, IF THE DRAWING FAILS TO SHOW THE INTENDED TYPE OF MOVEMENT, THEN ANY NUMBER OF MOTION LINES WILL NOT HELP. ON THE OTHER HAND, IF THE POSE YOU HAVE CHOSEN IS PERFECT, THEN YOU MAY NOT NEED ANY MOTION LINES TO INDICATE MOVEMENT.

FALLEN

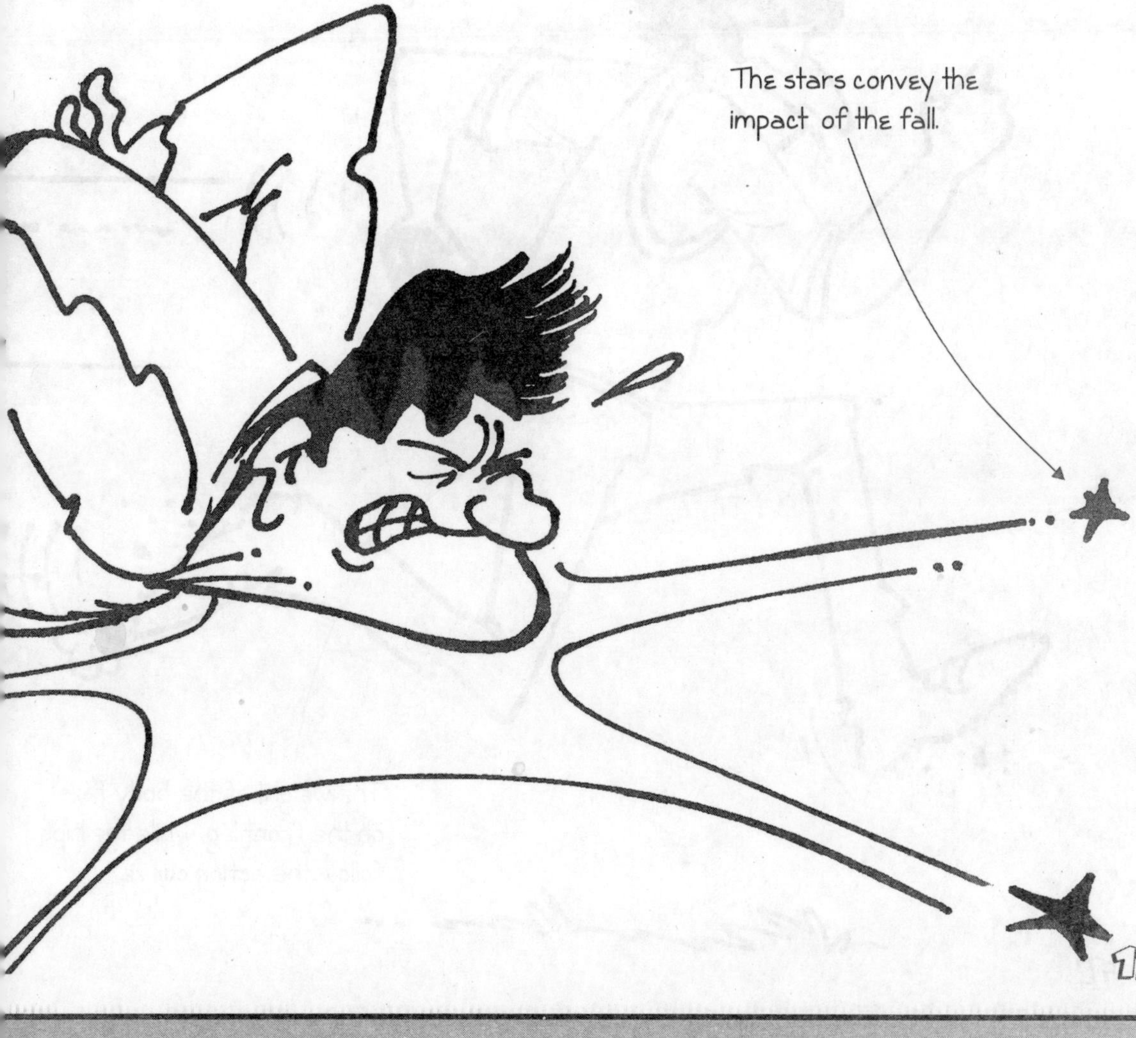

RUNNING

The flowing hair not only reinforces the movement, but also indicates his direction of movement.
The arms and legs of the figure move in a rhythmic manner in opposite directions to show the running movement.
The weight of the body falls on the front leg, while the hips follow the action curve.

Here, a bird is shown thrown off course.

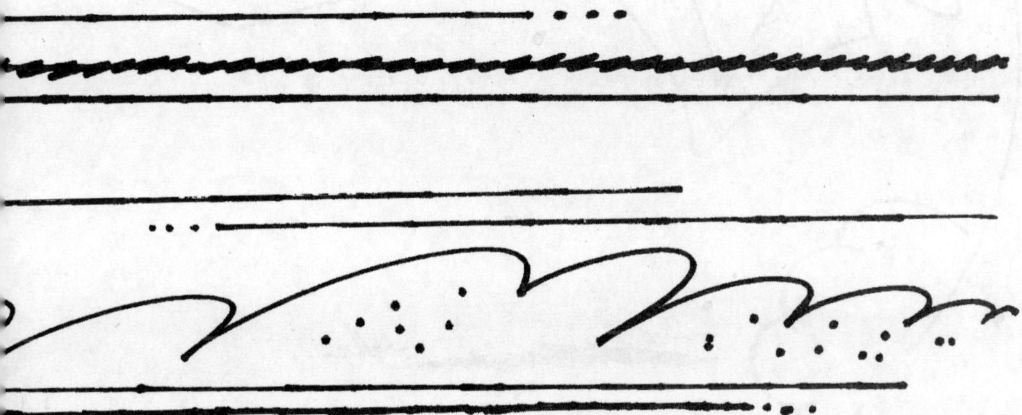

The speed lines with the dust clouds heighten the swiftness of movement.

CATCHING

This is a free-falling tilted body, suspended in space.. The shadow highlights the lack of contact with the ground.

DIRECTIONAL MOVEMENTS

ANOTHER WAY TO INDICATE MOTION IS DIRECTIONAL SOUND. THESE WORDS ARE USUALLY ASSOCIATED WITH ACTION. CONSIDER THE ACTION BEFORE DESIGNING THE LETTERING THAT BLENDS INTO THE ILLUSTRATION.

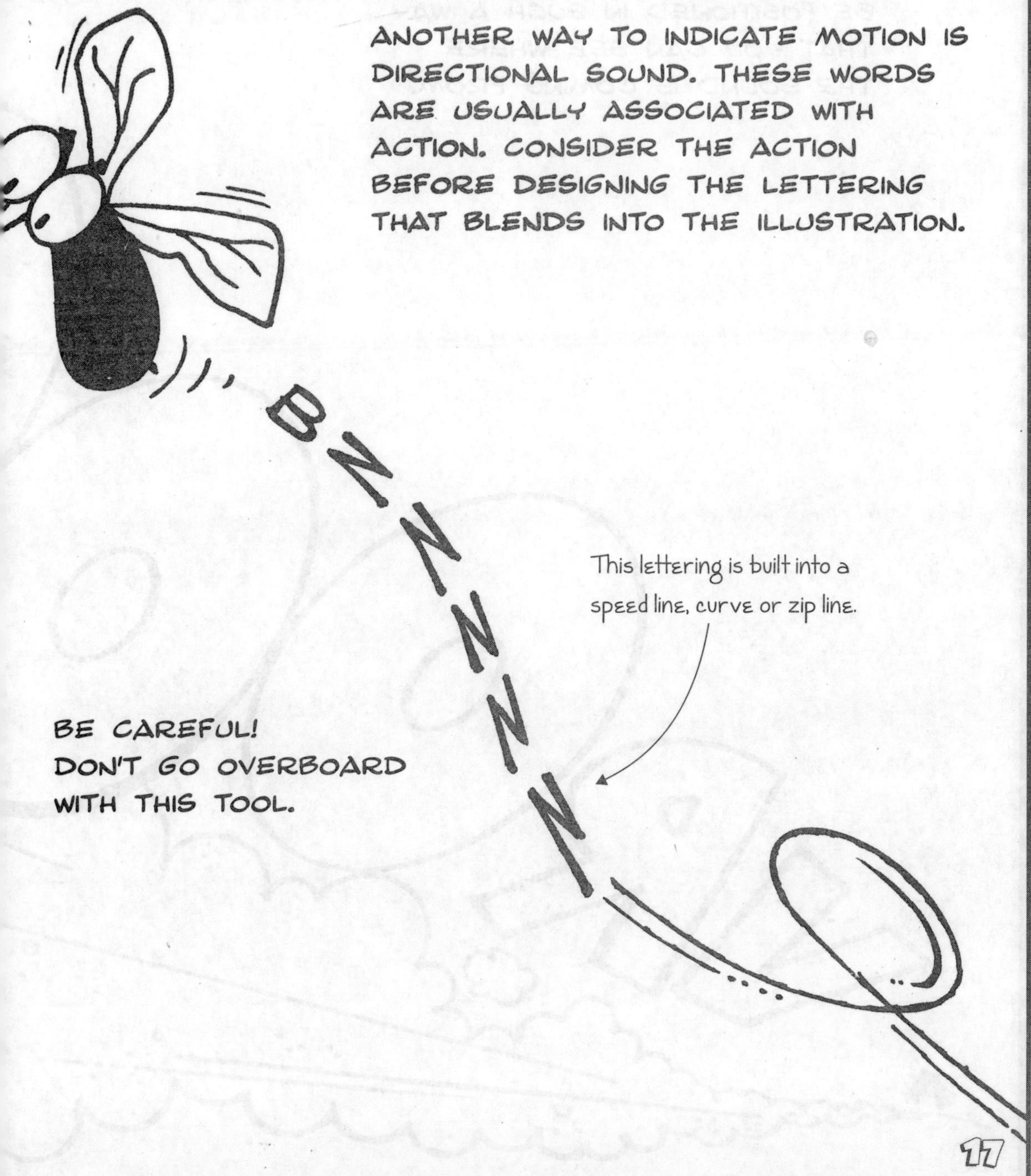

This lettering is built into a speed line, curve or zip line.

BE CAREFUL!
DON'T GO OVERBOARD
WITH THIS TOOL.

THE SOUND LETTERING SHOULD BE POSITIONED IN SUCH A WAY THAT YOU CAN SEE WHERE THE SOUND IS COMING FROM.

SUCH STYLISED LETTERING FOR SOUND CAN BE COPIED FROM COMICS, AND ONCE YOU HAVE UNDERSTOOD HOW TO DO IT, YOU CAN BEGIN TO DESIGN YOUR OWN.

MOVEMENTS WITH REASONS

YOU CAN ONLY DEFINE A MOVEMENT PROPERLY WHEN THE READER IS ABLE TO RECOGNISE THE REASON BEHIND THE OUTCOME.
IF THE READER IS UNABLE TO INSTANTLY UNDERSTAND WHY A SEQUENCE IS PORTRAYED IN A CERTAIN MANNER, THE IMPACT OF THE JOKE OR THE MESSAGE MAY BE LOST.

TO MAKE THE ACTION CLEAR, YOU COULD USE PROPS AS AN EXTENSION OF THE BODY. THIS WILL HELP YOU EXAGGERATE THE POSE.

YOU SHOULD START BY DRAWING ROUGH SKETCHES OF REAL-LIFE SITUATIONS AND SHOWING PEOPLE INTERACTING WITH OBJECTS. LATER, TRY TO EXAGGERATE THESE ACTIONS.

CARRYING

When the backward lean is exaggerated, the pose highlights the heaviness of the load along with the expression of anguish on the face. The dust that falls out of the box provides the required touch of humour.

CAUTIOUS

The figure implies withdrawal. The controlled and cautious movements heighten the joke and highlight the surprise element.

STARTLED

The frozen and immobile figure appears helpless, while the rolling pin thrown at him becomes the focus of the cartoon.

THROWING

The figure is stretched back, far enough for one leg to be lifted up, while the other bends due to the weight of the body.

The **ball is the force** behind the **action and the pose** indicates the distance to be travelled by it.

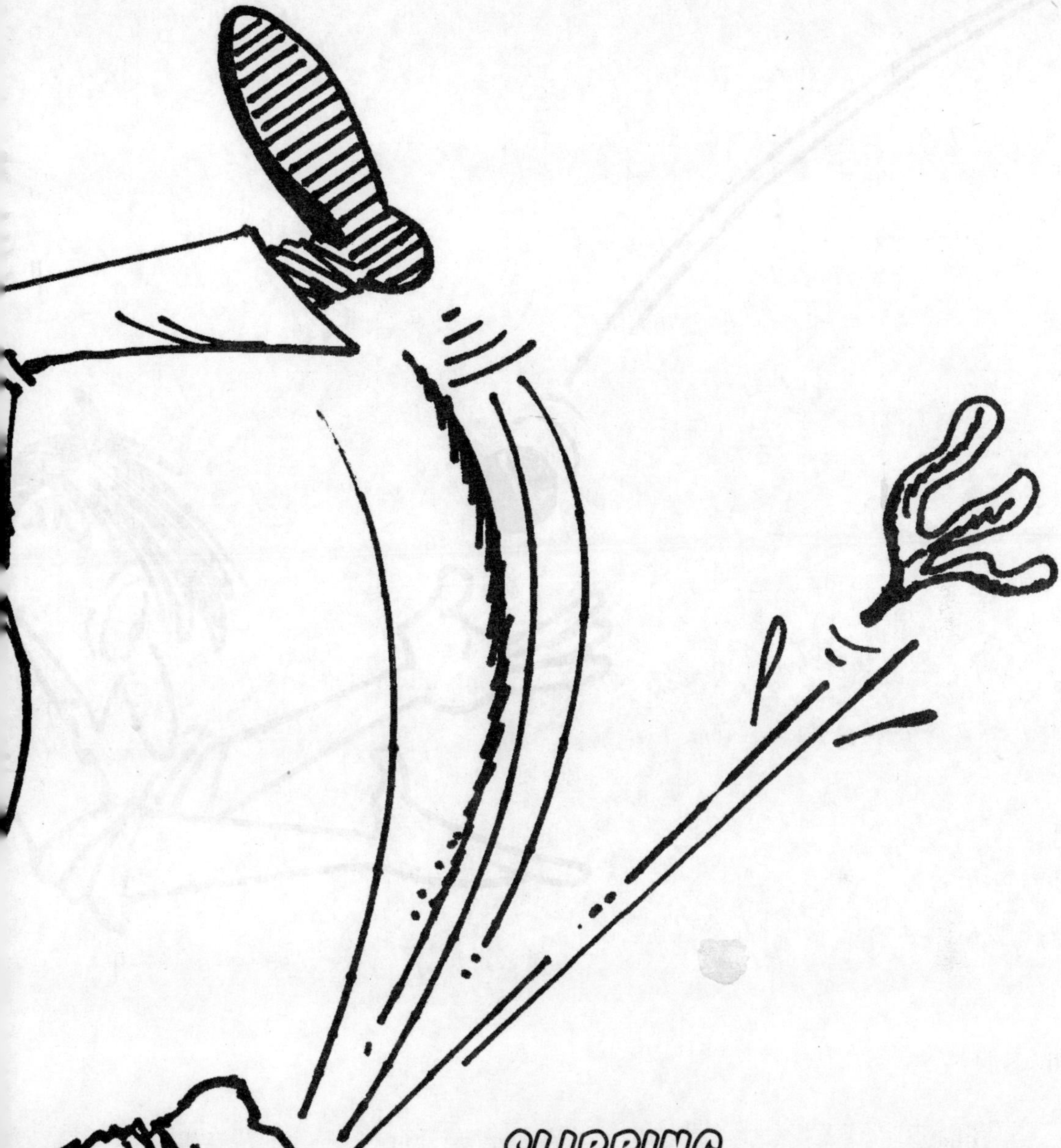

SLIPPING

The body is shown slipping, with a clear arc being formed by the back and the pelvis.

It is important to show the banana peel, which tells you why the man slipped, and where the centre of the action lies.

CATCHING

The figure leaps forward in anticipation of the catch, while the ball falls along a defined path.

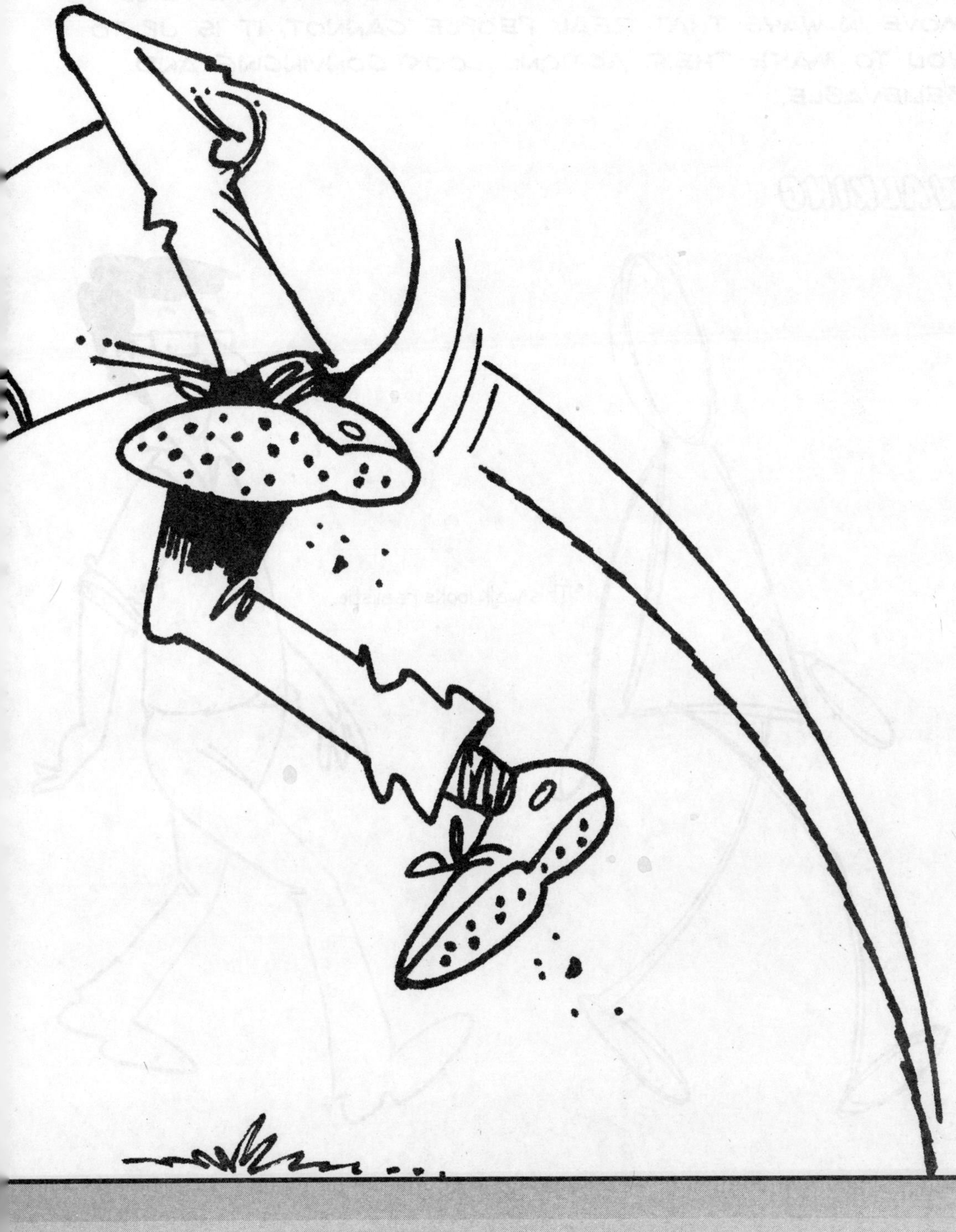

ACTION POSES

ACTION POSES ARE NOT ONLY INTENSE BUT ALSO FUNNY. ALTHOUGH IT IS POSSIBLE FOR CARTOON CHARACTERS TO MOVE IN WAYS THAT REAL PEOPLE CANNOT, IT IS UP TO YOU TO MAKE THEIR ACTIONS LOOK CONVINCING AND BELIEVABLE.

WALKING

This walk looks realistic.

OBSERVE ACTUAL MOVEMENTS OF REAL PEOPLE, THEN SIMPLIFY AND STYLISE THEM ACCORDING TO YOUR CARTOON.

RUNNING

The lengthened legs enhance the effect of frenzied/frantic running.

JUMPING

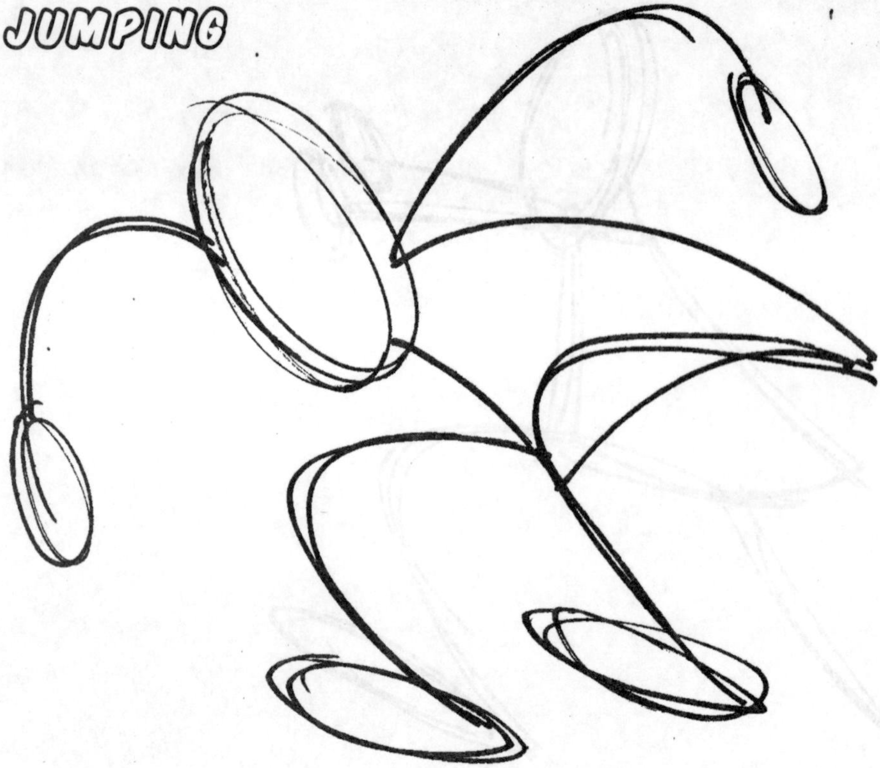

The figure's body weight is resting on the hands and the legs are up in the air to emphasise the jump.

DISTORTIONS

DISTORTION IS AN IMPORTANT TOOL USED BY CARTOONISTS TO GIVE A LARGER-THAN-LIFE QUALITY TO IMAGES.

THE HUMAN FACE AND BODY CAN BE DISTORTED TO CREATE MORE INTERESTING AND COMICAL CHARACTERS. THESE TECHNIQUES ARE USED FOR ANIMATED CHARACTERS ALL THE TIME.

DISTORTION OR EXAGGERATION MUST BE APPLIED CAREFULLY TO COMMUNICATE AND ENHANCE THE COMIC EFFECT MORE FORCEFULLY.

FACIAL DISTORTION

An elongated nose creates the impression of a tall, skinny person.

A wider and broader nose implies that the person is a tough character.

Eyes popping out of the character is just an exaggeration, as they go back to normal when he recovers from his excitement.

These bulging eyes suggest greed.

Highly animated and extended pouting lips show exaggerated love.

An enlarged, yelling mouth with a comically distorted tongue signifies anger or frustration.

BODY DISTORTION

YOU CAN DISTORT BODIES AND USE ABRUPT FORESHORTENING TO CONVEY MOOD AND MOVEMENT IN ACTION PICTURES.

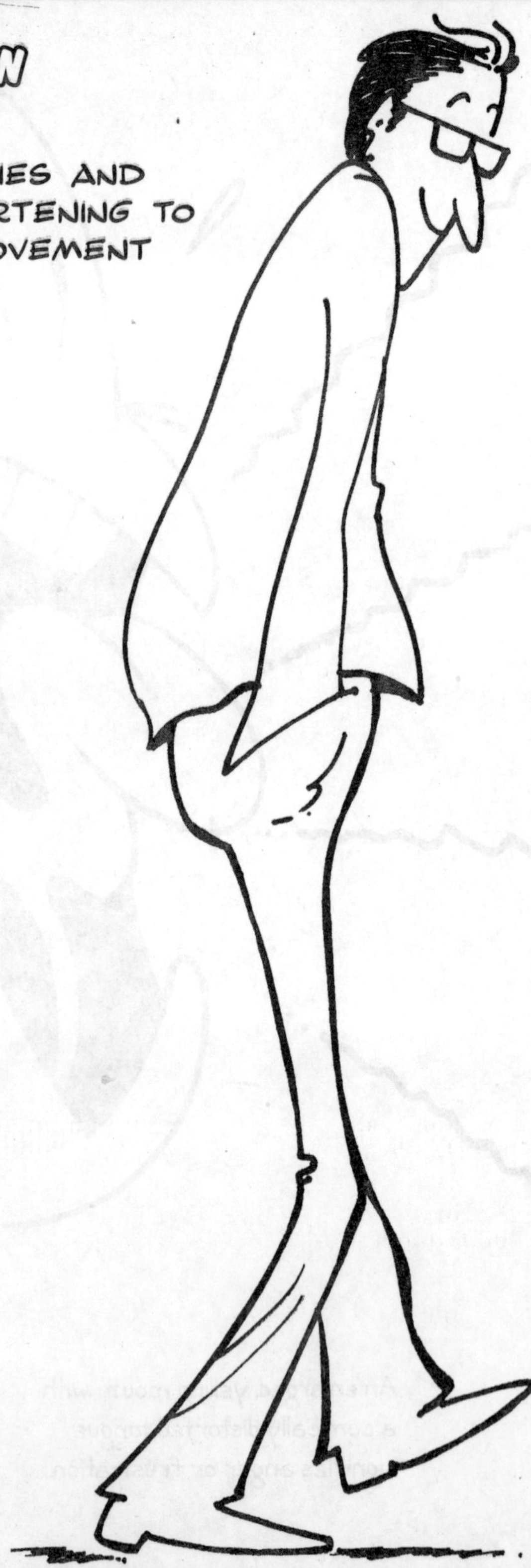

Excessive lengthening of legs creates the effect of a tall person.

Shortening the legs and torso, with bulky arms, gives the impression of a tough character.

Exaggerated and stretched legs show that the character is being chased. or is chasing someone.

Outstretched arms and legs and a character lifted off the ground suggests a startled expression.

ANIMALS IN MOTION

YOU CAN CHOOSE REALISTIC, CARTOONISH OR DISTORTED MOVEMENTS IN ANIMALS, BUT MAKE SURE THAT THEY REFLECT ANIMAL AS WELL AS HUMAN NATURE WITH EASE.

LET YOUR IMAGINATION RUN FREE.

Basic running pose.

Another running pose.

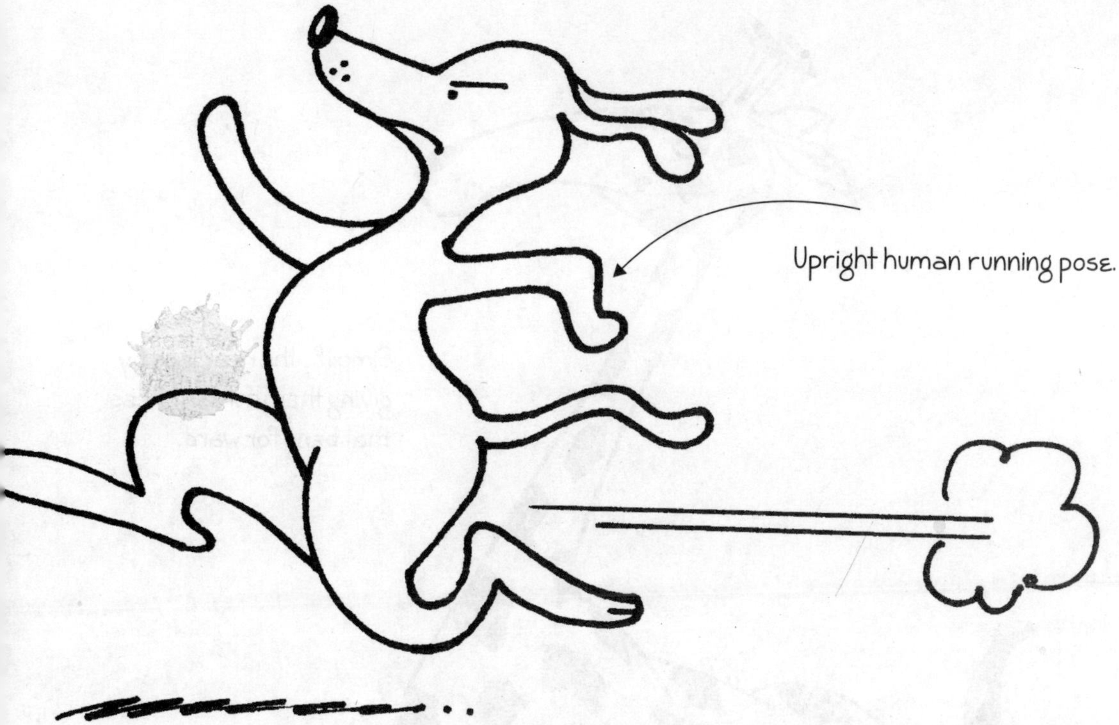
Upright human running pose.

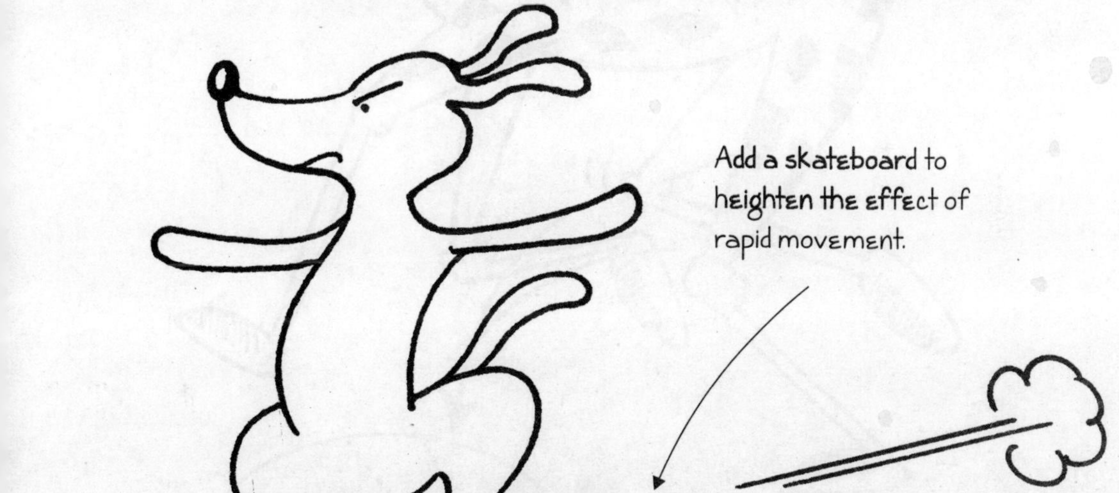
Add a skateboard to
heighten the effect of
rapid movement.

Simplify the rear legs by giving them human knees that bend forward.

With the body weight equally thrown onto both sides and the hands and feet placed appropriately, you can depict an elephant breaking into a run, just like humans.

Horses are fun to draw
in the cartoon world.

Horses don't really run this way with their hind legs forward and front legs back. However, in case of cartoons, the sillier, the better.

INANIMATE OBJECTS

ALMOST ANY OBJECT CAN BE BROUGHT TO LIFE BY ADDING FACIAL FEATURES, ARMS AND LEGS ON ITS SURFACE.

THE OUTER APPEARANCE OF AN OBJECT CAN SUGGEST PERSONALITY. FOR EXAMPLE, A PLIER CAN SUGGEST A TOUGH OR FORCEFUL CHARACTER, WHILE A PIECE OF BREAD CAN IMPLY A SOFT AND CUTE ONE.

JUST DISTORTING THE OBJECT WILL NOT DO. FOR EXAMPLE, YOU CAN TRY TO SHOW THAT THE PLIER IS IN MOTION.

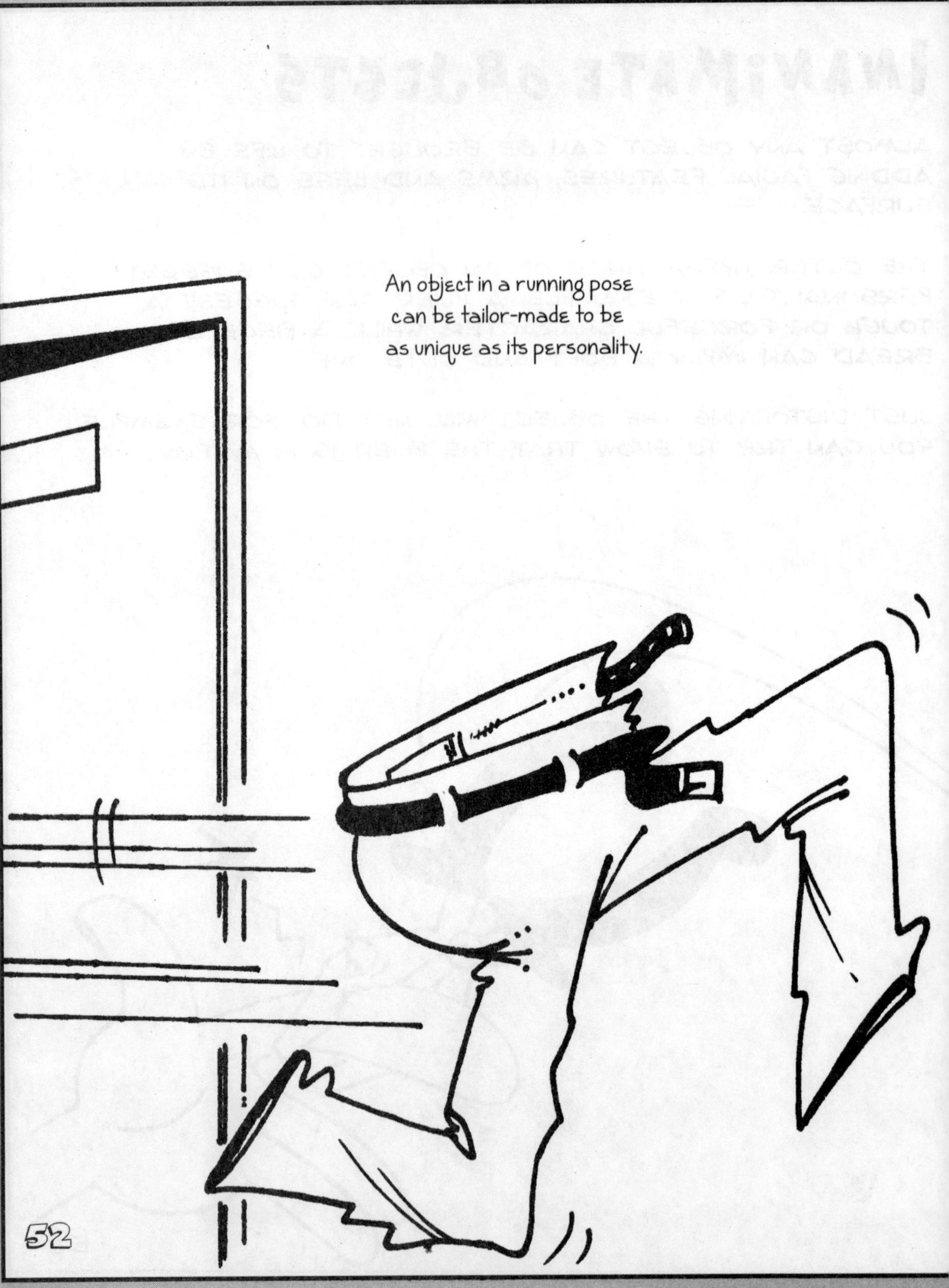
An object in a running pose can be tailor-made to be as unique as its personality.

SPEECH BALLOONS

SPEECH BALLOONS COMMUNICATE NOT JUST WORDS BUT ALSO DIFFERENT VOLUME LEVELS AND VOICE TONES.

STYLES OF SPEECH BALLOONS ARE DICTATED BY THE NATURE OF DIALOGUE OR CONVERSATION WITHIN.

External dialogue is enclosed within a word bubble with the pointer angled towards the speaker's face.

A rounded square speech balloon is a common way of showing normal speech.

A cloud-like thought balloon can be used to show thoughts in both words and pictures.

A jagged edged speech balloon denotes a dramatic outburst.

A speech balloon with dotted lines indicates a whisper.

SPECIAL EFFECTS

CARTOONISTS HAVE DEVELOPED A WIDE RANGE OF VISUAL SYMBOLS OR VOCABULARY TO SIGNIFY DIFFERENT EMOTIONS AND STATES OF MIND. SOME OF THE POPULAR EFFECTS ARE ILLUSTRATED BELOW, BUT IF YOU HAVE A BETTER IDEA OF PORTRAYING AN EMOTION, GO FOR IT!

REMEMBER, THESE EFFECTS ARE SUPPOSED TO LOOK CASUAL. SO, MINIMUM DRAWING FOR MAXIMUM EFFECT IS THE MANTRA.

Radiating sweat beads, conveying the idea of a worried or a hardworking person.

Upright, vertical lines are drawn around the head to symbolise shock or surprise.

Little circles or star bursts show a drunken or dazed state of mind.

Thundercloud with a lightning bolt to depict annoyance.

Wavy lines running through the body suggest shivering.

Sweat beads flying off, and a hanging tongue suggest exhaustion or someone suffering from the heat.

A violent impact is depicted with stars and the person's teeth falling out of the mouth.

Duplicating the images with lines depicting movement can create an effect of frenzied motion.

Jagged lines exaggerate the mishap of electrocution ...

... or a splash of water.

The shadow under the scooter and
the angle of the wheels convey that the
object is in motion.

It looks like this person is cycling at a normal rate,
but to add speed and movement ...

... distort the cycle. This also provides a comic effect.

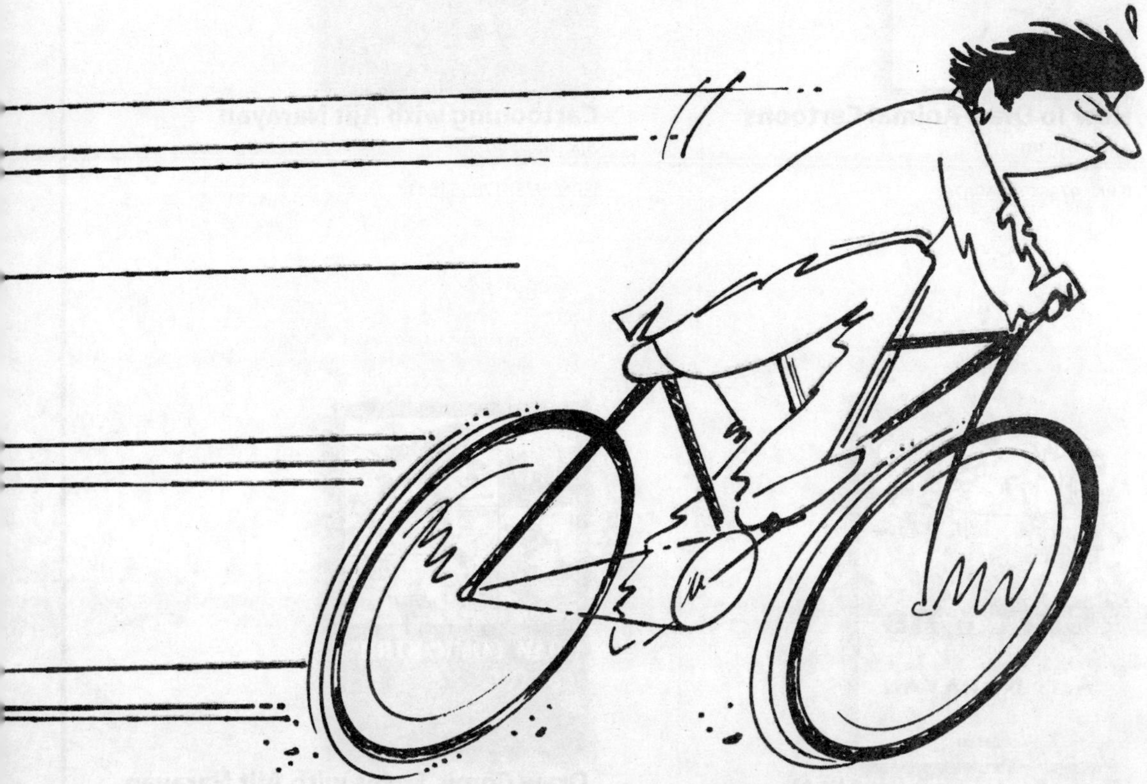

HAPPY DRAWING!

I HOPE YOU HAVE ENJOYED READING THIS BOOK AND IT WILL HELP YOU DRAW CARTOONS THAT COME ALIVE.

Other books by this author

How To Draw Animal Cartoons
Ajit Narayan

ISBN: 9788176559676

Cartooning with Ajit Narayan
Ajit Narayan

ISBN: 9788176554541

Draw Cartoons with Ajit Narayan
Ajit Narayan

ISBN: 9788184778557

Draw Comic Strips with Ajit Narayan
Ajit Narayan

ISBN: 9789351030065